Dear Parent:

Congratulations! Your child is taking the first steps on an exciting journey. The destination? Independent reading!

STEP INTO READING® will help your child get there. The program offers five steps to reading success. Each step includes fun stories and colorful art. There are also Step into Reading Sticker Books, Step into Reading Math Readers, Step into Reading Phonics Readers, Step into Reading Write-In Readers, and Step into Reading Phonics Boxed Sets—a complete literacy program with something for every child.

Learning to Read, Step by Step!

Ready to Read   Preschool–Kindergarten
• big type and easy words • rhyme and rhythm • picture clues
For children who know the alphabet and are eager to begin reading.

Reading with Help   Preschool–Grade 1
• basic vocabulary • short sentences • simple stories
For children who recognize familiar words and sound out new words with help.

Reading on Your Own   Grades 1–3
• engaging characters • easy-to-follow plots • popular topics
For children who are ready to read on their own.

Reading Paragraphs   Grades 2–3
• challenging vocabulary • short paragraphs • exciting stories
For newly independent readers who read simple sentences with confidence.

Ready for Chapters   Grades 2–4
• chapters • longer paragraphs • full-color art
For children who want to take the plunge into chapter books but still like colorful pictures.

STEP INTO READING® is designed to give every child a successful reading experience. The grade levels are only guides. Children can progress through the steps at their own speed, developing confidence in their reading, no matter what their grade.

Remember, a lifetime love of reading starts with a single step!

Step into Reading, Random House, and the Random House colophon are registered trademarks of Random House, Inc.

Visit us on the Web!
StepIntoReading.com
randomhouse.com/kids

Educators and librarians, for a variety of teaching tools, visit us at RHTeachersLibrarians.com

ISBN: 978-0-449-81437-6 (trade) — ISBN: 978-0-375-97158-7 (lib. bdg.)

Printed in the United States of America
10 9 8 7 6 5 4 3 2 1

nickelodeon

DORA the EXPLORER

DORA AND THE UNICORN KING

Adapted by Ellie Seiss

Based on the screenplay "King Unicornio"
by Rosemary Contreras

Illustrated by Victoria Miller

Random House 🏠 New York

Hi! I am Dora.

This is Boots!

We take a walk.

We meet our friend

Unicornio.

There is a door.

We see a rabbit

with a letter!

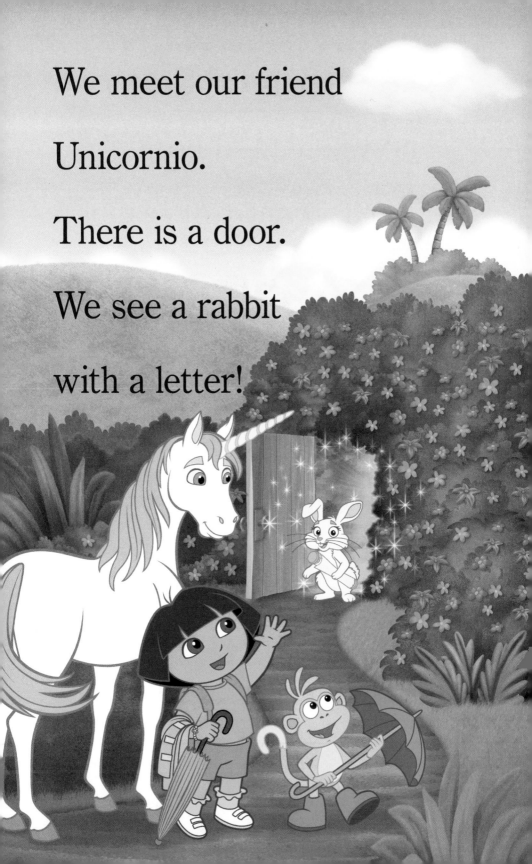

The letter is for Unicornio.
The Enchanted Forest
animals want Unicornio
to be their king.

We must go

to the castle and get

Unicornio's crown!

But Unicornio thinks
he is not kind, smart,
brave, or strong,
like a king.

We can show Unicornio

that he can be a king.

How do we find the castle?

Map says we need
to go through
the Riddle Tree.
We need to go past
the volcano.
Then we will be
at the castle.

On our way to the
Riddle Tree, we see elves.
One is too small.
He cannot
reach the peaches.

Who can help the elf?

Unicornio!

Unicornio is kind,

just like a king.

We make it

to the Riddle Tree!

We need to answer

the tree's riddle.

Who can solve the riddle?

Unicornio!

Unicornio is smart,

just like a king.

There is the volcano.
There is a dragon, too.

Unicornio makes a shield
with his horn.

We need to stomp our feet
to make a really big shield.

We make a big shield.

It stops the dragon!

Unicornio is brave,

just like a king.

Near the castle,
we see a squirrel
in the river.

We help

the squirrel.

Unicornio saves the squirrel!

He is strong,

just like a king.

23

Unicornio is kind, smart, brave, and strong.

He is a true king!